presenting...

Wenda!

BENJAMIN brown books

Copyright © 2008 by Christopher Kennedy

Benjamin Brown Books

All rights reserved. No part of this publication may be reproduced, stored in a retrieval system or transmitted in any form or by any means, electronic, mechanical, photocopying, recording, or otherwise, without prior written permission from the publisher. For further information, contact Benjamin Brown Books, at #121- 3495 Cambie Street, Vancouver, BC, V5Z 4R3. Visit our website at www. benjaminbrownbooks.com.

Illustrations and cover design by Emily Mullock
Typesetting by Meghan Spong

Library and Archives Canada Cataloguing in Publication

Kennedy, Christopher Aslan, 1968-
  Wenda the wacky wiggler / Christopher Aslan Kennedy.

(The rainbow collection)
ISBN 978-0-9782553-2-9

  I. Title. II. Series: Kennedy, Christopher Aslan, 1968-
Rainbow collection.

PS8621.E632W46 2008   jC813'.6
C2008-905638-8

Printed in China by Everbest

08 09 10 11 12 5 4 3 2 1

This little light of mine, I'm gonna let it shine...
let it shine, let it shine, let it shine!

— For Enentsa, my love, my earth, my moon

Wenda loved to laugh and
dance and feel herself move.
She'd wiggle with joy
and let herself groove.

She always kept moving
to each kind of beat—
even while sitting,
she'd be tapping her feet.

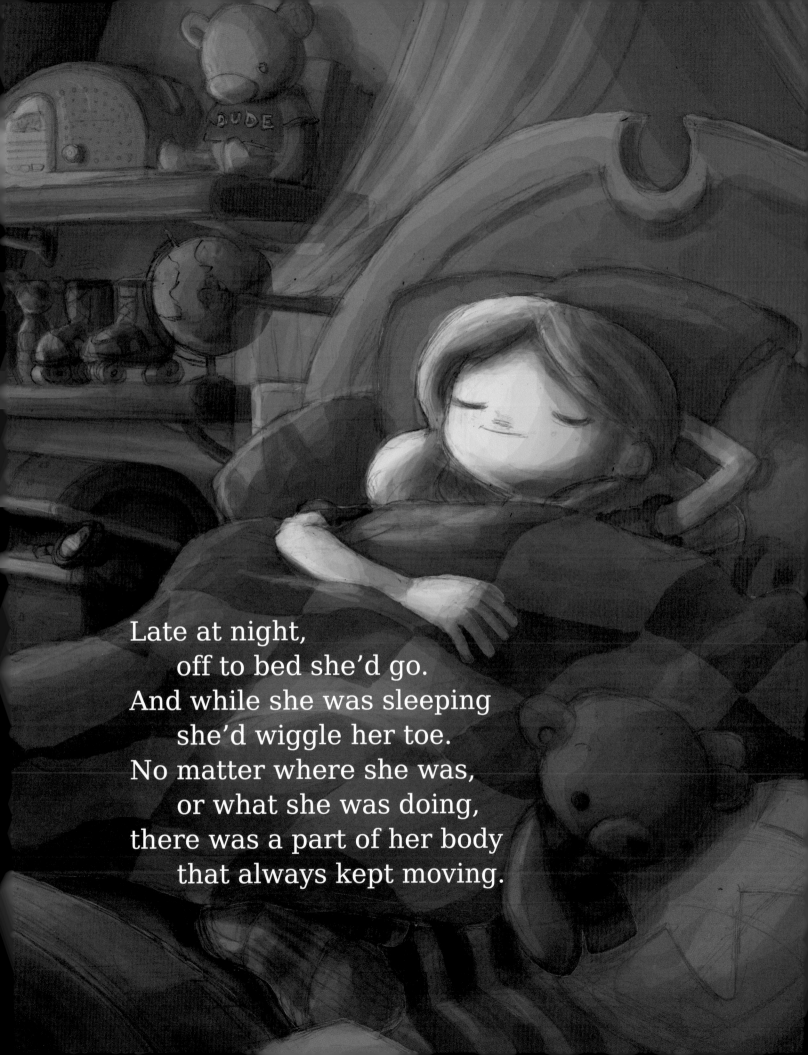

Late at night,
  off to bed she'd go.
And while she was sleeping
  she'd wiggle her toe.
No matter where she was,
  or what she was doing,
there was a part of her body
  that always kept moving.

The people in her town were grumpy and grey,
so Wiggling Wenda was told not to stay.
People were cranky and seemed kind of mad;
they couldn't see the joy that Wenda had.

The mayor didn't like it when she whirled into town,
it made people grouchy when Wenda came 'round.
"We will stop all the music!" yelled the mayor in disgust.
"And Wiggling Wenda will stop bothering us!"

The people were ready when she came the next day,
there was no music to cause Wenda to sway.
Everyone stared as she got out of her car—
hoping the silence would drive her a-far.

Wenda started to move
like she always did,
and laughed out loud
like a little kid.
"How can this be?"
asked the mayor of the town.
"There's no music at all,
there's none to be found!"

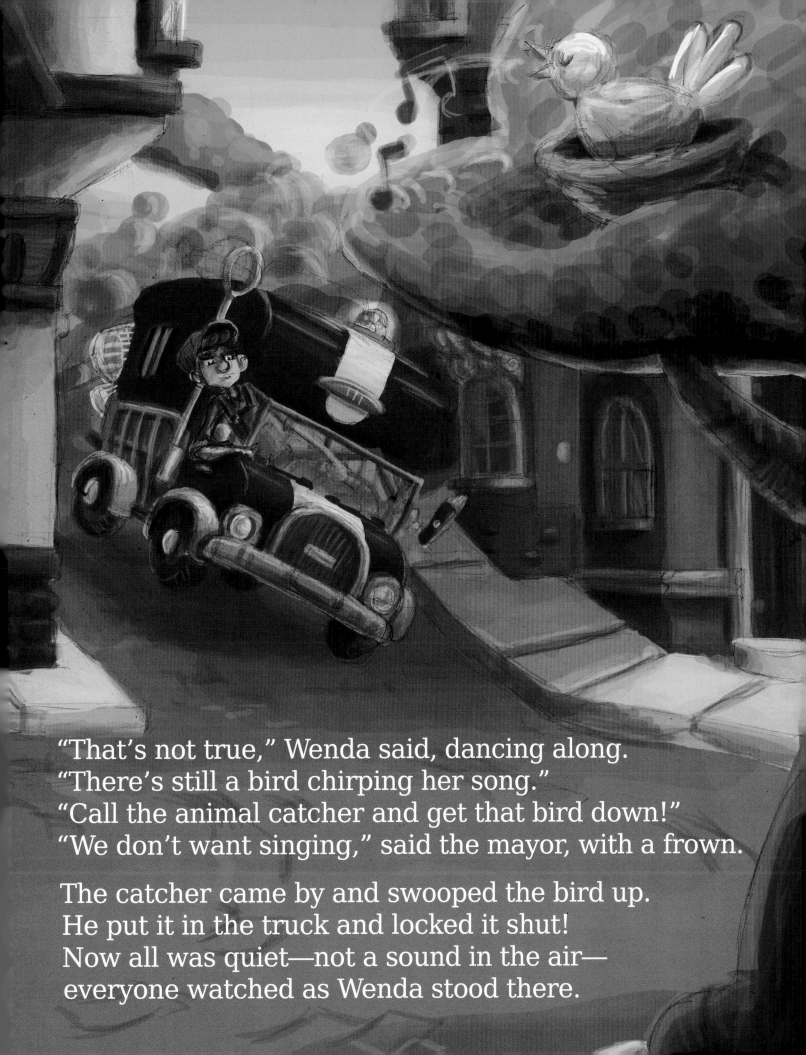

"That's not true," Wenda said, dancing along.
"There's still a bird chirping her song."
"Call the animal catcher and get that bird down!"
"We don't want singing," said the mayor, with a frown.

The catcher came by and swooped the bird up.
He put it in the truck and locked it shut!
Now all was quiet—not a sound in the air—
everyone watched as Wenda stood there.

No music, no sound—no beat to be found.
"That's it," sighed Wenda, "I guess it's all gone.
'Cause without any sound, there can be no song.
I will never again have the same chance
to express to the world my love of dance."

"Humph!" said the mayor. "It's finally stopped."

Wenda slumped to the ground, she felt like a rock.

It was silent and still;
no one dared move.
Wenda was quiet.
It was the end of her groove.

But lo and behold,
to the people's surprise—
Wenda's foot started to move
and began to rise!

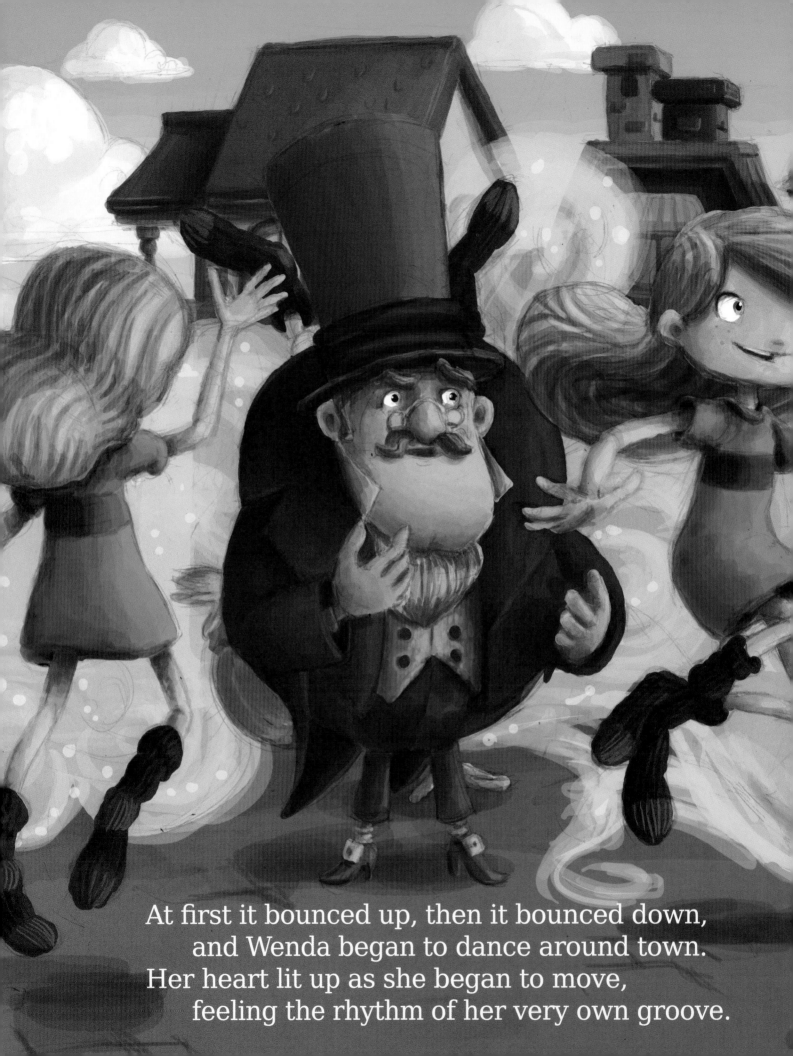

At first it bounced up, then it bounced down,
and Wenda began to dance around town.
Her heart lit up as she began to move,
feeling the rhythm of her very own groove.

"Ha- ha!" she laughed, it felt so good
to move and to groove like she knew she could.
"Impossible!" said the mayor. "There's nothing to be heard;
not a sound, not a peep, not even a bird!"

"That's why," said Wenda,
    as she wiggled along,
"it's quiet enough
    to hear my own song!"

"It was there all along!"
    she shouted in stride.
"The music I hear,
    it comes from inside!"

It feels so good, so good to be me,
with music inside that's forever free!
It's the same for you, too, just give it a chance—
So let your song out and do your own dance!

Your song is unique in each of your hearts,
and once it sings it will never depart.
One by one the people's hearts lit up
(and the bird was freed from the animal truck).

Their eyes had a sparkle;
    their hearts began to shine.
The gift they had forgotten,
    they'd had all the time.
The teacher did The Twist,
    and the baker did The Bump.
They all began to boogie,
    and the mayor shook his rump.

"I am love!" said Wenda,
    dancing her song.
"I knew it! I knew it!
    I knew all along!

We all have wisdom,
    a love deep inside,
Our own inner knowing,
    our very own guide.

They began to relax and let their love flow.
It was a breath of fresh air from feeling so low.

We can share this love
    in all that we do…
in our work, our family,
    and our friendships, too!

We are grateful to Wenda for shining so bright,
for now we remember, we are each our own light!

From ear to ear,
   Wenda kept grinning,
She knew this dance
   was just the beginning.
And so they expressed
   from deep in their hearts.
They spoke and wrote
   and created great art!

from the heart,

to the heart,

for the heart